For Mimi,
who, through all our changes,
held us tight.

Copyright © 1989 by Betsy James. All rights reserved.
Book design by Julie Noyes   Printed in Hong Kong.
Library of Congress Cataloging-in-Publication Data
James, Betsy. The red cloak / retold and illustrated by Betsy James.
    Summary: In this free retelling of an old Scottish ballad, Jan,
who is convinced her friend Tam is not dead but has only
disappeared, follows the advice of a wise old woman and with the
help of a red cloak releases him from capture by elves.
    ISBN 0-87701-564-3
    [1. Fairy tales.   2. Folklore—Scotland.]   I. Title
PZ8.J217Re 1989   398.2′1′09411—dc19   88-22603
                                                     CIP AC

10 9 8 7 6 5 4 3 2 1

Chronicle Books
275 Fifth Street
San Francisco, California 94103

The RED CLOAK

Betsy James

Chronicle Books · San Francisco

Long enough ago
and far enough away,
in a village by a lake,
two children were born
on the very same day:

a girl named Jan
and a boy named Tam.

They played together,

they grew up a little,

and they loved each other very much.

But then,
very early
one midsummer morning
before the sun was up,
Tam stole out all alone.
He went to fish for minnows
near the stones
by the lake—
and he never came back.

His family looked high
and his friends looked low,

and everyone looked in the lake,
but they never found him.
"Poor Tam!" they said.
"He's dead."
"He's not!"
cried Jan.
"I won't listen!"

And she wouldn't.

A whole year passed.

Still Jan said,
"My Tam's not dead!"
Nobody believed her.

So when midsummer eve
came round again,
Jan said,
"Then I'll find him myself!"
Off she went
to the wisest old woman,
to ask how to begin.

"What do you want?"
said the wisest old woman.
"I want my friend!"
said Jan.

"It's hard to be a friend,"
said the wisest old woman.
"It's harder still to lose one,"
said Jan.

"That's what you think,"
said the wisest old woman.

"My Tam's not dead!"
said Jan.
"That he's not,"
said the wisest old woman.
"The elves have stolen him."

"Then I'll steal him back,"
said Jan,
"and that's that!"

"You'll do what you'll do,"
said the wisest old woman.
"But remember what I tell you.
Go all alone
this midsummer night
to the stones at the edge
of the dark lake.
When the elves pass
you'll see your Tam
on a tall white stallion.
He has been sleeping for this whole year.
Leap up then
and drag him down.
Throw this red cloak round him
and, no matter what happens,
hold him tight!"
"I will," said Jan.
"Thank you!"

She took the cloak,
and off she went home.

In the middle of the night,
Jan rose, and crept
out of the still house,
down to the stones by the lake.
She waited, listening,
until, at almost midnight,
she could hear the elves.

They came in a procession,
proud and pale.
First among them,
on a tall white stallion,
rode Tam, asleep.

Jan leaped up
and dragged him down.
She threw the red cloak round him,
and held him tight.

The elves raved and raged,
but they dared not go near
the red cloak.

Tam changed into
a lump of ice
and froze her,
but Jan held him tight.

He changed into
a blazing flame
and burned her,
but she held him tight.

He changed into a lion.
He changed into a dove,
but still she held him tight.

He changed into
a snake,

a fish,

a turtle,

a rabbit,

and a tiny ant,
but still
she held him tight.

He changed into
a bar of red-hot steel!
But still Jan held him tight,
wrapped in the red cloak,
and leaped with him
into the cool dark waters
of the lake.

With shrieks and wails
the elves vanished into mist.

When the sky cleared,
it was midsummer morning.
Tam lay in the water,
sleepy and smiling,
just waking up.
"Why, Jan!" he said.

"Why are you *holding* me so tight?"